MICA MCDONALD

CONFLICT: AN ANTHOLOGY

BLUEROSE PUBLISHERS
India | U.K.

Copyright © Mica Mcdonald 2024

All rights reserved by author. No part of this publication may be reproduced, stored in a retrieval system or transmitted in any form or by any means, electronic, mechanical, photocopying, recording or otherwise, without the prior permission of the author. Although every precaution has been taken to verify the accuracy of the information contained herein, the publisher assumes no responsibility for any errors or omissions. No liability is assumed for damages that may result from the use of information contained within.

BlueRose Publishers takes no responsibility for any damages, losses, or liabilities that may arise from the use or misuse of the information, products, or services provided in this publication.

For permissions requests or inquiries regarding this publication, please contact:

BLUEROSE PUBLISHERS
www.BlueRoseONE.com
info@bluerosepublishers.com
+91 8882 898 898
+4407342408967

ISBN: 978-93-6452-399-8

Cover design: Daksh
Typesetting: Sagar

First Edition: September 2024

Acknowledgements

I would like to take a moment to express my deepest gratitude to my family and friends for their unwavering support and encouragement throughout the writing of this book. Their love, understanding, and patience have been the core of my creative journey. I am eternally grateful for their belief in me, especially in the times I nearly gave up. This book would not have been possible without their love, persistence, and support. Thank you from the bottom of my heart.

Contents

SMILE FOR THE CAMERA 1
    Harry 2
    Robert 10
    JJ 14
    Harry 16
    JJ 19
    Sasha 21
    Julia 23
    Sasha 24
    Harry 25
    Charlie 27
    Harry 28
    Charlie 31
    Harry 34
    Julia 35
    JJ 39
CONSEQUENCES 45
    Smile For The Camera Epilogue 46
MENTAL 57
THE PERSONAL BLOODSHED 67
    The Mental Prequel 68

SMILE FOR THE CAMERA

Harry

"Come on, it will be fun!" Charlie says, pointing at the large poster on the primary school gate that reads 'Thriller Escape Room' followed by a 'large cash prize'. JJ immediately agrees after hearing that. Honestly, the cash prize looks highly tempting, so I agree.

"Puzzles are my thing. It will be easy," Robert stated.

"But it says it will be live-streamed; I don't think I want to be on camera", Julia muttered.

"Just put this on over and save the audience having to look at it." JJ laughed as he rested an empty paper bag on her head.

"Hey, quit it, JJ. It will be fine, Julia. you can stick with me if you would like." Sasha flicks the bag and puts an arm around Julia.

"Well, that settles it. Let's go," I say, pushing the gate open. All six of us walk into the empty school. You would think other people would jump at the chance of free money, especially for something as simple as an escape room.

"Nobody else can ruin our chances now," Robert says, taking the poster from the gate.

We arrive at what seems to be a reception area. It smells fresh and new—maybe it was recently built. Robert points to an arrow that leads to another door. I'm starting to feel strange. Usually, people briefly explain the escape room before it begins. Everyone motions for me to go first. I hesitate before pulling the door open lightly.

We are met by a staircase with arrows leading to the top. Thankfully, the stairs are small and easy for most of us to climb. As we reach the top, Robert pants heavily with his hand on the wall, asking us to wait between his heavy breaths. Sasha puts an arm around his shoulder and helps him walk with us while JJ laughs.

I open the door and see a large hall. It looks different to what I was expecting. Many pictures cover the walls: maths equations, seasons, art, music and more. In the centre of the room is a table with a monitor on top of it. I guess it makes sense for things to be all digital. We all walk closer, and six watches rest in front of the monitor. A stack of paper also reads 'Waivers ' on the top. The monitor turns on, and a shiny arrow points down at them. Charlie immediately puts them on, followed by JJ.

"What are you guys waiting for?" JJ snarled. "You're not chickening out, are you?" He was talking to the rest of us, but his eyes fell heavily on Robert, whom Sasha still held up. He quickly walked towards the table and put them on. The rest of us did the same.

We all take one of the booklets.

"Aren't waivers one of those things used in places you can die, like bungee jumping?" Julia states, slowly backing away.

"Well, if it's going to be live-streamed, it's probably just to say we allow ourselves to be filmed," Robert says as he begins to sign it. I flick to the last page and sign it, too.

After everyone has signed it, we stack them back on the table. The monitor flashes, and then a countdown appears. It began at five and quickly dropped to zero. Everyone just stared at it. Nobody spoke.

"I thought there would be an explosion or something," Charlie laughed.

"Don't even joke about that", Julia squealed as she clung to Sasha.

"This 'escape room' is a joke. I bet there's no prize money either," JJ snarled as he started to take off his watch. Just then, there was a bright flash of light.

My eyes open slowly. Pain erupts in my brain as I sit up, and my eyes ache as they try to adjust to the lights. I look around and notice that we are no longer in the hall. I'm in a classroom. Children's drawings are messily slathered across the walls, and the tables are in a neat semi-circle around me. I notice everyone else walking around the classroom, looking in drawers, on shelves, under tables, and even behind some pictures.

"What's going on?" I asked.

"Good morning, sleeping beauty", JJ mocks as he continues to rummage through a drawer.

"There's a key in here somewhere. We need to find it. The money is on the line here," Charlie says. He climbs on a chair and looks at the top of a bookshelf. I guess the escape room has already started. Why was I asleep then?

"Are you just going to sit there, or are you gonna get off your ass?" JJ snapped, stopping his search to stare daggers at me. There's no point dwelling on it. We have some money to win.

After what feels like forever, I want to give up, and I'm not the only one. We all sit down in the centre of the room except JJ.

"How has nobody found the key yet? Robby, you're meant to be the big brain here. Where is it?" JJ yells.

"Stop calling me Robby", Robert retorts.

"We have searched everywhere. Are we going to be trapped here forever?!" Julia cries, hugging Sasha.

" Come on, guys, don't give up yet. Let's do one sweep of the room again, then go from there," Sasha encourages. We all stand up again and begin searching. Then, my leg starts to irritate me. I itch it and feel something solid in my pocket. I pull it out and see that it's a key— the key we have been looking for all along.

"Harry had the key the whole time!" JJ yelled. Everyone's eyes fall on me. The silence was deafening, but it didn't last long. Charlie started bursting out laughing.

"To think we were about to give up when he had it all along," he said. JJ stormed towards me and pushed me. I quickly lost my balance and fell backwards onto the table.

"You just wanted to keep all the money to yourself, didnt you?" JJ questioned angrily.

"Hey, I didn't know it was there!" I stand up and push JJ back, but I move further back than he does. He stares at me dead in my eyes before beginning to approach me. Charlie suddenly puts an arm around us, still laughing his head off.

"Come on, guys. It's not like you to retaliate, Harry. Anyways, it's been found; now let's go!" Charlie enthusiastically takes the key from me and walks towards the classroom door, unlocking it. He does an exaggerated bow with his arm extended toward the exit.

"Go on, Harry," JJ patronises as he pushed me toward the door. "You're the 'leader' of the group, so… Lead'" I stand in the doorway and look at what seems to be the same hall we got the watches from. I see the monitor is still there, but it's rotated towards us. The papers, however, are gone. I take a deep breath. Everyone has formed a line behind me. They all give me encouraging smiles and thumbs-ups (except for JJ), so I step out into the hall as they follow close behind.

I approach the centre of the room. A loud whirring sound echoes in the hall, and the monitor flickers on. A dark figure appears on the screen, followed by a pre-recorded applause.

"Hello, my name is Proxy. Congratulations on finding the key. Was it difficult?"

"Well, actually-" Julia begins.

"An audience vote will decide the next challenge! While that is going on, I will explain something." The voice was distorted and barely understandable. It gave me quite an unsettling feeling.

Just then, somebody walked into the hall. They were wearing masks covering their mouths and hats covering everything above their eyes. In his hands was a giant camera pointed directly at me.

"How many challenges are th-"

"You all have a cameraman that only you can see, thanks to those necklaces you have on. They will follow you and ensure you're not breaking the rules. The audience will also be watching you through these cameras." I reach a hand up to my neck and feel the cool metallic necklace around me. I don't know how I didn't notice it before. It's tight as hell.

Everyone exchanges enthusiastic glances while waiting for the 'audience vote' to conclude.

"This is going to be easy," JJ says.

"Yup," Charlie agreed, resting his arm on JJ's shoulder.

"As long as certain people don't try to do anything shady… or get in the way." He looks over at Robert this time.

"Shut up, JJ. If anything, your temper is the biggest hindrance to us all." I sigh.

"At least I'm-"

"Guys, come on. You're embarrassing us in front of all these people." Charlie pats both of our backs lightly and waves to his camera.

"What's the matter? You're usually more level-headed than this," Sasha whispers to me. She has a good point, I don't usually entertain JJ's bullshit. I don't know why he is suddenly getting to me now.

"The results are in. The first game is Tag. It will last ten minutes. To tag someone, you must touch them and say "tag" simultaneously. The audience will choose the first tagger. The last person to be the tagger will be eliminated. By audience vote, the first tagger will be Robert."

"Eliminated, tag? What kind of thriller escape room-" Julia begins before she is quickly cut off.

"Everyone will have 30 seconds to run, then the tagger will be after you. Ready?"

"No", Julia sighs.

"Set, go!" A timer replaces the dark figure on the screen. JJ immediately takes off running, laughing and mocking Robert as he goes.

"Good luck, Robby. You're going to need it." He darts through the door and runs down the stairs out of sight.

"Don't listen to him, Rob. You've got this." Charlie pats his back and runs in the same direction.

"Yeah, I believe in you!" Sasha hugs him quickly and drags a reluctant Julia to the back staircase. Robert hangs his head and fiddles with his hands. I put my hands on his shoulders and tried my best to reassure him.

"I know Brawn isn't your thing, but you're smart. I know that; you know that; everyone knows that. So, play to your true strengths." He gives me a comforted smile and gives me a thumbs up. With ten seconds left on the screen, I run down a third staircase.

Robert

I watch the timer near its end and get ready to run. I feel like the audience knows I'm the slowest in the group. I think about what Harry told me. I have to play to my strengths. The timer reaches zero, so I walk towards the staircase JJ went down. I'm going to prove to him that brains can beat brawn.

I look at the cameraman who is walking next to me. His eyes stare blankly at me as we walk through the double doors and down the stairs.

"So… how long have you been a cameraman?" I try to break the silence, but my question is ignored. I awkwardly wave at the camera as I arrive at a door. Suddenly, my watch vibrates.

"DOOR OR STAIRS?" slid across the tiny screen, followed by a 10-second timer. Another vote? I guess it will help with my indecisiveness. I stand by the door and wait for the timer to tick to zero.

"DOOR" slides across the screen, so I place my hands on the green door and push it open. A blinding light engulfs my vision, and the wind gently grazes my face. I look around at the large playground with multiple apparatuses scattered across it. Near the end of the playground, I see JJ lying at the top of a slide, his arms folded comfortably across his chest. I don't think he heard me come out outside.

I walk down the concrete staircase and creep towards the slide. I hear him sigh loudly, so I hide behind a narrow tree. He sits up and stretches dramatically.

"You're skinny as hell, but that tree aint coverin you." JJ laughs. "I noticed you the moment you stepped outside." I walk out from behind the tree and watch him walk down the slide. I slowly walk closer to him but he doesn't move; he just smirks at me. I stop about 5 feet in front of him. The condescending grin that's plastered across his face stabs my chest. Why am I even trying? He's 100 times faster and stronger than me. There's no way I'll be able to catch him.

"Don't give up." The sincerity in JJ's voice took me by surprise. Does he actually want me to do well? Maybe he does care about people. "If you give up too easily, it won't be worth rubbing in your face later when you lose!" He will never change. Laughter erupts from his mouth as he hops over the side of the slide and takes off running towards the building. Without a second thought, I chased after him. An unnerving irritation built up inside of me and forced my body forward. My body immediately aches, but I don't care. I have to catch him. My mind is clouded as I mindlessly follow JJ like a shadow. He constantly looks back at me, laughing and even runs backwards. My vision blurred, and all the pain I felt in my body disappeared.

"Come on, Robby!"

Catch him.

"Aw, you nearly got me that time."

Catch him.

"Come on, don't give up, you're so close."

CATCH HIM!

My thoughts were painfully loud. Those two words echoed repeatedly. They struck my brain with a pain I've never felt before. I hate this emotion. I want it to stop. I feel out of control. My body won't listen to me anymore. It just keeps chasing him. We go upstairs, through corridors and hallways, but I don't stop. I can't see or hear anything but JJ's smug face and stupid remarks. Nothing else matters; I just have to catch him. I can feel the fatigue catching up quickly and start slowing down.

"It's not your fault you're shit at everything you do, Robby."

Something in my head snapped. I dive forward and grab his leg, causing us both to tumble at the top of the staircase. My head slams against the floor, but the pain only lasts for a second. Before I knew it, my fist connected repeatedly with JJ's face. My vision is completely blurred, and I feel nothing but rage. I punch him again and again. My feelings begin to weaken, and my head starts spinning. My breathing is sporadic, and my heart tries to stab its way through my chest.

JJ smirks and looks up at me. Condescension fills his eyes as he sits up slightly.

"You done? You're as weak as ever. You landed how many hits, and none fazed me, even slightly. But don't worry, buddy. The best way to learn is through experience." In a split second, JJ punched me on the side of my face, making me fly backwards. The shock left me paralysed on the ground as I watched JJ stand up and tower over me. He stamps down on my stomach several times, chuckling to himself. A cough forces its way out of me, and I struggle to breathe. Tears fall effortlessly down my face immediately as my stomach feels like it's being impaled. He crouches down next to me, and a maleficent smile stains his face.

"You're a disgrace, y'know that? I don't know how any of the others tolerate you." He presses his fist down into my stomach. The pain forbade me from speaking. My mouth is open, but no words come out, not even a scream. I want to disagree, but I can't. I want to fight back, but I can't. I can only lay there. I can tell he's wanted to do this for a long time. The eagerness in his eyes strikes fear into me, one I've never felt before. He raises his fist and smiles wide. I close my eyes and brace for impact.

BEEP BEEP!

BEEP BEEP!

BEEP BEEP!

My wrist vibrates lightly. I open my eyes slowly. JJ looked at his watch and laughed again.

"You didn't say tag." The realisation hit me harder than a ton of bricks. I caught him, but I didn't tag him. My watch went red, and JJ's watch went green. I lost. I'm out.

𝓙𝓙

I didn't think he would catch me; that could have gone very badly. I look down at Robby's distraught face and can't help but be thankful that he lost. Upbeat music and applause begin to be heard from the speakers. It feels like it's just for me. I did do the most out of all of us, after all. I stand up and soak it all in. Another victory. Another excellent ego boost.

My thoughts come to an abrupt halt as a sharp scream cuts through the applause.

It's Robby.

He writhes around on the ground, tears flowing quickly down his face. He claws and scratches at his neck. He looks almost possessed. Blood starts to pour down like a waterfall.

What?

What is happening?

Is he messing with me?

I should ask him what's wrong and try to help, but my feet stay plastered on the floor. He looks me in the eyes, his screams beginning to get drowned out by the applause still playing. Then he speaks quietly, but I still hear him. I wish I didn't.

"Help me…" My body refuses to move. I can only watch in horror at the scene unfolding before me. He says it a few more times, his voice getting quieter by the second.

Then it stops.

He stops.

My mind stops.

Harry

The beeping of my watch brings me to a sudden halt. It flashes green, and applause plays from the speakers above. This "escape room" is so easy; the prize is ours. I wonder who lost, though. I have faith in Robert.

I walk to the middle floor and see Julia, Charlie, and Sasha talking and laughing in the centre of the room. As I get closer, they all look at me, their faces tense with anticipation, so I give them a thumbs up. Charlie laughs and high-fives me as we talk about how easy the game was.

Then, we hear the sound of someone running down the stairs at a scary pace.

"They do know the match is over, right? I mean, I thought the applause was a good indicator." Charlie says as he skips towards the staircase. He swings the door open, and JJ comes running in, knocking Charlie over. JJ stands there, clinging to the door, breathing extremely heavily. Extends a hand to Charlie, helping off the ground

"Sorry, sorry," he says frantically. Everyone looks at each other in confusion.

"Are you good? You look very-"

"Robert! He's dead."

The room falls silent for a moment, and then Charlie starts laughing,

"No way. Did he catch you or something?"

"Or did you do something to him!" Julia accuses.

"I will prove it to you. Hurry up!" He turns around and begins bolting up the stairs. Sasha is the first to follow him, panic filling her eyes. The rest of us follow hesitantly. We don't want to believe it, but it's possible.

At the top floor, another deafening silence washes us away.

"That wasn't fucking funny," Sasha says, punching his arm.

"Don't worry, I thought it was quite funny. Your acting skills are top-notch," Charlie laughed as he put an arm around JJ.

"This doesn't make any sense. HE WAS HERE! Robert was…" JJ trails off as he kneels in the centre of the room, mumbling quietly.

"Robert? You can come out now. The joke is over," Julia shouts out.

"He probably left already, and I don't blame him. That's a lot of money to lose because of Tag," I say, trying to keep any order. Everyone looked at JJ for confirmation, but he didnt move or speak. I know he didn't like Robert, but this was going too far. I had to put an end to his sick joke.

"Congratulations!" A robotic voice booms from the speakers. "You made it past the first game. The next game will be chosen by audience vote, so be patient."

"Come on, guys, let's be positive. We've got this." Charlie eased the mood. We began chatting and laughing, waiting for the next game.

A loud chime sounds from the speakers, "The next game is Red Light, Green Light. All you have to do is make it to the end of the hall within the time limit, and you pass. Red lights me stop, and green means go. If You move when the light is red, you return to the start. Simple. Good luck."

We all go to one side of the hall, and excitement floods the air. A timer begins to count down from 10.

"Something doesn't feel right. I think we should leave. About what JJ said, I-" Julia whispers to me. The screen turns green, and we all run forward. Charlie leaps ahead, JJ a close second. The rest of us are relatively in line with each other.

JJ

Charlie skips ahead confidently. My mind is fighting itself, guilt and determination. I can't allow myself to lose. I can't die. If they don't believe me, that's on them. I can do this alone. I don't need anyone else to survive. I pace myself while keeping in front of the rest of them. I won't risk being last.

The light turns red, and I freeze. Charlie somehow manages to end up on one leg but doesn't move. The light stays red for a while, allowing my heart to return to a normal rhythm. I try to calm my brain.

I can do this alone.

I don't need them.

I don't need anyone.

The light turns green again, and I begin to walk forward. Within a second, it turns back to red, and a loud thud echoes in the hall.

"Julia to the beginning." The voice says. That doesn't surprise me; she's an emotional wreck even though she doesn't believe what I said about Robert. None of them did so they could find out for themselves.

The game progresses. I focus, ignoring the others' joy. Charlie glides around in front of me, freezing perfectly every time. He's strangely athletic, so he could probably be useful in the future.

Charlie passes the line first and begins cheering everyone else on. Time slows down as I reach the line and turn around. Julia is at the beginning, and she's not moving.

This may be a good thing. I disliked her the most. She doesn't deserve to win this. I do—only me.

Sasha

I'm only a step away from the line. Two minutes quickly tick down. We can all win this together.

My heart stops as I see Julia at the beginning, sitting down with her head on her knees and shaking violently. JJ's earlier claim plays like a broken record in my head.

She can't die. She can't.

"Sasha, back to the start." The voice echoes from the speaker as I raise my hand. I run back to the start, ignoring everything else. Julia's head rises. Her eyes are red, and tears flow effortlessly down her face, making tears threaten to fall from mine. I won't let her go alone. I sit down next to her and wrap my arms around her.

"What are you doing? You need to go," she cries, trying to push me off.

"I'm not going without you", I reply, holding her tighter.

"Don't be stupid!" She quickly stands up and begins pulling me forward—a minute left. The red lights feel longer than before, but we get closer and closer. The line is only a few steps away.

Ten seconds. Red light.

Five seconds. Red light.

Panic fills my body. What if we don't make it? Will we actually die? I shouldn't have come back. I should have crossed the line when I had the chance. I should have-

BEEP BEEP BEEP.

What.

BEEP BEEP BEEP.

When did the light turn green? I failed Julia. I feel my hand get squeezed. Our hands are still connected. I smile weakly at her. I have to apologise. I ruined her chances of winning and possibly her chance at life.

"I-"

"I'm sorry, Sasha. It's all my fault!" Julia interrupts me. Tears flow like a waterfall from her eyes. I realised where I was standing. Our hands are connected, but we aren't on the same side of the line.

She made it. Good. She's safe.

Julia

Sasha smiles at me as she squeezes my hand gently. She's still comforting me even though she lost. I feel so guilty. I should have dragged her past the finish, but I didn't realise she wasn't paying attention. Apologies spill rapidly out of my mouth. I can't stop. I want to comfort her, but I can't move. My mind is moving at lightning speed but feels disconnected from my body; it refuses to listen.

Sasha

My head starts pounding. Everyone's mouths are moving, but I can't hear anything they say. My legs ache, so I allow myself to fall to the floor. The pain begins to increase, and my brain feels like it is being electrocuted and stabbed. I yell and scream, but I don't think my pleas reach anyone. Everyone's distraught faces look down at me. I try to stop, but I can't. I feel like I'm making them suffer just as much as I am.

Warmth suddenly grips my heart. Julia is kneeling next to me, holding me up. It feels like the pain stops for a second as she hugs me tightly. Her sobs began to drown out mine as I felt a stab in my neck. I struggle to move my hands, and my voice falls silent. I can't scream anymore. Her face fills my blurry vision. I think her mouth is moving, but I can't hear anything she's saying. Why is this happening? I can't console her anymore. I want to tell her it will be ok. Is this what dying feels like?

"...I promise." What did she promise? I can't hear. My vision fades slowly. I wish I could console her one last time. She's a mess without me.

Harry

What the hell is going on? She's stopped moving. Maybe she passed out or fell asleep?

"Do you believe me now?" JJ's condescending tone brought me back to reality. I should have listened to him and made us leave. Is this my fault? Are Robert and Sasha dead because of me? It's all my fault.

"JJ, shut the fuck up right now. I don't want to hear it. You didn't even try to make us leave. You're selfish and mean and- Fuck" Julia stammers and bursts into tears again. JJ's taken aback by her outburst and steps back. Charlie tries to make light of the situation but struggles to get a single word out.

"We need to leave right now." I walk towards the exit but don't hear footsteps behind me. I turn around and see JJ holding Charlie's arm, stopping him from taking a step.

"Do you want to get us all killed?!" I storm up to JJ and try to release his grip on Charlie.

"I'm not letting this opportunity go because you're too much of a bitch to play some games. Robbert died because he was weak, and Sasha died helping the weak. I don't know about you, but we aren't weak." He pushes me away and drags Charlie to the centre of the room.

"Jules, let's go." I grab her hand and try to pull her up, but she doesn't let me. She retracts her hand away from me and cradles Sasha.

"I can't leave. I promised Sasha I would win the money for her, so that's what I will do."

"You're joking, right?" What is wrong with them? They just witnessed a murder, and they want to keep playing. I should just leave without them.

Charlie

I'm staying? Why am I staying? This was meant to be fun. I wanted us all to get along for once. This group was hanging on by a thread, so I thought doing something fun would help, but no joke could help this situation. JJ seems confident, and I trust him, so I should be, too. I can't give up; I must help them see the positive side. Somehow.

Harry

I watch them all go to the centre of the room, waiting for the next game. I can't leave them, can I? I can't live knowing I allowed them to risk their lives like this.

"Guys, please think about this properly. Do you think Sasha and Robert would want you to throw your lives away like this?" I try to reason. They all stare blankly at me momentarily, like I said the stupidest thing ever.

"Harry, it will be okay. We know what to expect, and if we all work together, we can do this easily," Charlie reassures me. I always envied his carefree nature and ability to turn any situation around.

Reluctantly, I join them all in the centre of the room. Julia hugs me. I can't witness another death, so I will protect them all.

"What an… unexpected turn of events. Make your way to the top floor for the next game," the distorted voice echoes from the speakers. Everyone silently walks towards the stairway and makes their way up. I think for a moment before reluctantly following them.

I walk through the double door to the centre of the room with everyone else. Julia smiles weakly at me,

"Thank you for staying with us."

"Yeah, well…" I struggle to find the right words; this situation is far beyond my comprehension, but if everyone wants to continue, I have no choice.

"The next game will be musical statues! You all know how it works; I don't need to explain. However, you have three lives to last you ten minutes. There are also no rules. Good luck." The voice booms over the speakers. Nobody speaks, but everyone looks at JJ.

"Don't do anything reckless, JJ", I warn. He stares at me blankly, then smiles,

"As if I would do anything. It's like you don't even know me." He laughs and turns to Charlie.

"I think we should stay far away from them", Julia says, pulling me closer to the edge of the room.

The music starts, so I sway slowly. It's hard to get into the mood, knowing that moving could kill you. Julia smiles encouragingly at me as she tries to move my arms a bit more.

The music stops, and everyone freezes instantly. I hold my breath as fear threatens to take over my mind. I need to survive. I can't let them down. The speaker chimes, and the voice speaks again,

"If I don't get more enthusiasm from you guys, I'll take a life away from you all!" How do they expect us to dance like we didn't just witness our friend get murdered in front of our eyes?

Charlie and JJ have no problem with it, and Julia starts moving with dedication. I need to, as well, for all of them.

The game goes on for what feels like forever.

Dancing.

Stopping.

Dancing.

Stopping.

This is quite tedious. Is musical statues the way I bargain my life away? What sicko decided to do this to us? They need to get some serious help.

Charlie

I know my life is on the line, but I can't help but enjoy myself. I shouldn't be having this much fun, but for some reason, I am. This doesn't feel normal.

It doesn't matter. It's better than being stressed like Harry and Julia seem to be. She seemed very determined earlier, but I guess she can't go against her personality. JJ is having fun, though, which is quite strange. I like this side of him, though. I've always tried to get him more involved with our group, which I think made us actual friends, as much as he wants to deny it. Deep down, I know he truly enjoys our company, but the others don't give him a chance. I hope the rest of us get out, and we can all start again. I think we could all get along very well after this.

"You all lose one life. JJ isn't dancing properly." I see Harry and Julia glare at us. It may take longer to get us all closer, but I won't stop trying. Tears start to fall from Julia's eyes. I think the stress is getting to her; maybe I can encourage her more and pass on my optimism to counter her pessimism.

I start to walk towards her, but JJ grabs my arm,

"She's fine. Focus on yourself," He says sternly.

"But she's-"

"Upset about Sasha, probably. But hey, if you worry too much about others, you will forget to worry about yourself." He lets go of my arm, so I step towards Julia.

"Another life is gone for Charlie and Harry", The voice announces.

"Told you," JJ says smugly as the music starts again. He was looking out for me; I knew he still cared. "Get them to come over here. We can finish this all together." This feels like what I've always wanted with our group. Although not everyone is here to enjoy it, we can still have fun.

I motioned for Harry and Julia to come to us, but they hesitated. I put my hands together pleadingly so they slowly dance to us.

"We can do this together, guys. Even JJ said so!" I dance more eagerly. I'm excited about what our group could come to after we get out. We can start going out more without excluding anyone, like nandos or funfairs. We could even go on holiday together. This will be so good! I'm glad.

I look over at the time hanging on the wall. It's in the final minute. One more minute till this is over. The game gets more straightforward as the music stops every 16 seconds. It's like the game master isn't trying anymore.

"Guys, it stops every 16 seconds" I shout.

Thirty-two seconds left. We can do it. I count down 16 seconds till the next pause. I've never felt more energetic in my life. This experience feels like a dream that forces you to see the silver lining. If it is a dream, I don't want to wake up.

I feel an intense pressure on my back. Everything slows down as I start to fall forward.

14 seconds.

My head slams into Harry's side. He turns and catches me, but we both lose our footing. The music stops, but we don't. My face slams on the floor, and my vision goes blurry. Maybe I was too excited. Where is the silver lining? I'm usually so good at finding it, so why am I struggling so much? Why am I struggling when it really matters? I have to find it.

I need to find it.

Harry

I can only let myself fall as Charlie's shoulder crashes into my side. The music stops, and the room falls silent until we hit the floor. I look up at Julia's troubled face. I don't even know what to do. I hope my eyes deceived me. I should have left when I had the chance. I can't die like this. I need to go, fuck everyone else. I need to get out right now.

Julia

JJ puts his foot back on the floor. How has this happened? I know they said no rules, but I didn't think we would actually have to worry about it. I should have listened to my gut and stayed away from him.

Harry frantically stands up, pushing Charlie off him roughly. He stares blankly at me. I should try to comfort him the way Sasha does for me.

"Save it," Harry says to me before turning around to face JJ's smug face. "You have some fucking nerve, you know that?"

"What happened?" Charlie stammers as he sits up.

"Your best buddy over here just got us killed, that's what." Venom fills Harry's voice, his face bright red, and his fists tightly clenched.

"No... you wouldn't do that, right JJ?" Charlie sounds like he's on the verge of tears. I walk over and hold his arm to get him up, but he doesn't move. Instead, he moves further away from me and closer to JJ, clinging onto his shirt like his life depends on it.

"Charlie, don't-" I try to lift him off the floor again.

"You wouldn't kill me on purpose, would you? Tell me he's lying." Charlie pleads as he pushes my hand away. JJ looks down at him, his face unreadable.

"Harry and… Charlie. You are eliminated," Proxy announced over the speakers. Silence once again fills the room. Charlie refuses to let go of JJ's shirts, waiting for an answer.

"Please…" Tears flow quickly down his cheeks as he finally lets go of JJ and sinks further to the floor. His body shakes violently as he sobs uncontrollably.

I've never seen him cry before. I've never seen him do anything but be happy and burst into fits of laughter. I don't know what to do. Sasha was good with stuff like this, but I don't know what I'm doing. I'm in over my head; I should have listened to Harry. I never should have promised Sasha.

"I would never do that to you on purpose. I lost my footing and bumped into you. You're my best friend, you know that." JJ kneels to Charlie's, resting his arms on his shoulders. Tears fill his eyes as he looks at Charlie's puffy ones.

"I knew you wouldn't." Charlie reaches up and hugs JJ tightly, nearly knocking him over. JJ hesitantly hugs him back, his face softening, and a look of guilt flashes across his face.

"I'm sorry", JJ whispers. Immediately after, Charlie's body tenses and starts to shake, but they keep a firm hold on each other. I turn around and see Harry stumbling towards the stairway. He's cursing loudly and clutches his neck. I go over to him as he falls to the floor and starts screaming. I can feel tears flood my eyes as I try to help him up.

"Fuck off, I should have left you all last game. This is all your fault." He weakly pushes me away and tries to continue moving to the stairs.

Is it my fault? Sasha is dead because of me. She risked her own life to save me; all she did was take care of me, and I couldn't do the same for her. I spent too much of my time being pessimistic, but it's like I can't help it. My mind feels like a grey cloud waiting to hail on me. I wish I had taken Sasha's place.

I look back and see JJ staring at me. He stands up, letting Charlie's body fall to the floor. He uses his sleeve to wipe his eyes, puts his hands in his pockets, and walks towards me. I instinctively move back; a fear I've never felt before makes my body feel like lead.

I keep walking back, and then my foot hits something solid. I turn around and see Harry's lifeless body sprawled across the floor. He's really gone. This place is fucking sick.

A lens fills my vision. The masked man holds the camera directly in my face as tears fall to the floor. I've only just remembered he was here filming for the livestream. People are still watching this. People are actually watching us suffer and die.

"What the fuck is wrong with you all?" I feel like bawling my eyes out, but only a few tears come out. I feel numb. This is all too much.

I feel a hand on my shoulder. JJ looks at me with a threatening gaze.

"We signed up for this. Get a grip and say your goodbyes." He immediately grabs my arm and pulls me towards the staircase, forcing me to step over Harry's body. Colourful arrows point upwards, so we make our way up. I don't even know what to say to him. Does he not feel any remorse?

Guilt?

Sorrow?

He caused this, and now he's walking away like it's nothing. He's a murderer.

"How could you-"

"Stop," JJ says quietly but sternly. His voice wavers slightly. Maybe he can feel emotion.

No. After what he just did, I don't think he's capable. He's probably just having an adrenaline rush. Meanwhile, I don't even know what to do with myself. I feel the very little strength I had in my body drain out of me as JJ effortlessly pulls me up the stairs with him.

We reach the top floor. JJ pushes the door open and pushes me in. He walks behind me like a prison guard. In the centre of the room, A monitor rests on a table. In front of the monitor are two small boxes. The monitor turns on, and the words "PICK A BOX" slide across the screen. JJ pushes me to the side and picks up both boxes, shoving one of them into my arms while keeping his eyes glued to the screen.

The monitor turns red, and then black text flashes on the screen.

Kill.

Kill.

Kill.

I open my box and immediately let it fall from my hands. The object clatters to the floor, and my hands start shaking.

JJ

Kill? Is this the final game?

I take the blade out of the box and turn it in my hand. I press my finger against it, watching as blood immediately drips to the floor. I look up. Julia stumbles backwards as she drops her box on the floor. Her hands tremble, and her breathing quickens. Tears form a puddle on the floor as she looks at me like a defenceless puppy. I hold the knife firmly in my hand and take a Step towards her.

"You're not seriously about to kill me, are you?" She falls to the floor and scrambles to pick up the knife, then points it at me.

"I'm not leaving here empty-handed, Julia. I've lost…" My words get caught in my throat. Their faces quickly flash through my mind, but one doesn't leave, and my body freezes.

Charlie. His carefree nature and willingness to always try to include me sticks in my brain like a nail. Why couldn't he have left me alone? Why did I let him drag me into this cursed friend group?

"JJ… Are you crying? Like, for real crying this time?" Julia's confused voice snaps me back to reality. I put my hand to my damp cheek in disbelief. I didn't even notice my blurry vision or stinging sensation. I'm crying. All because of him.

Don't hesitate.

Think about the money.

You don't even like her.

My brain is torn in half. I have to do this. I have to get the money. I have to win. It has to all be worth it.

"JJ, seriously, please think about this!" Her twitching hand holds the knife like it weighs a ton, and she uses her other hand to shuffle backwards as if she's in a horror movie. "I promised Sasha I would win for her." Her speech is stammered and broken as she tries to hold back the flood escaping her eyes.

"Then come and fucking kill me, Julia. Don't just sit and let me kill you because…" I feel my own words get caught in my throat again. I don't know why I'm struggling like this. These people never meant anything to me. That's true, right? I hated them all, didn't I? "You're not the only one that made a promise."

My mind is clouded. I quickly close the distance between us.

Help.

I crouch down to her level and point the blade at her.

Help.

"JJ, please listen to me!"

Help!

A choking cough echoes in my brain as I pull the knife out of her neck. Her eyes widen as she presses her hand against her neck. Her mouth opens, but no words come out. She slides down the wall, her body shaking and heaving violently. Blood spills from her mouth and neck as her eyes drain colour.

My hands start shaking like hers, and I drop the knife. I cover my ears and try to block her out. Her pleading eyes never leave mine, and guilt starts to seep into my body slowly. I squeeze my eyes shut tight, and after what feels like a century, I hear her body hit the floor. I turn around and open my eyes. The monitor turns green.

I really did it.

I won.

Pain suddenly erupts in my head. I immediately fall to the floor, and Julia's body is forced into my eye line. I feel like throwing up and crying, but my body allows neither. I hear footsteps walking behind me. I try to turn around. I try to do anything at all, but my consciousness fades.

A camera lens fills my vision.

"And now, the moment you have all been waiting for. The final vote!"

There is something different about the voice. It doesn't sound distorted by the monitor this time. Is it clear and close? My head is pounding, and my body forbids me from speaking, no matter how hard I try. A rope secures me tightly to something that only allows me to look forward into the camera.

"On the screen, you will see two choices. Live or die. If you choose live, JJ will continue in the show. If you choose the die option, he will get a slow but entertaining ending. "

This must be a joke. I won. I went through all of that for nothing? They are all dead because of these stupid games. I struggle desperately, but I can't move an inch.

"You have one minute to vote!" The camera moves further away from me, as does the person holding it, but Their face isn't covered like it was before. They smile earnestly at me and wave.

"Hey JJ, I guess I should give you that long villainous speech, right?" He laughs. My breathing turns sporadic. I can't believe it. I blink as fast as I can, hoping my eyes are deceiving, but he doesn't disappear.

"Robert?" I finally managed to speak. His smile faded, and he stared blankly at me for a moment.

"This really messed with you, didn't it?" He laughs again. "I'll keep it simple for you. You needed to be taught a lesson. I had the ability to teach you that lesson. I have the ability to keep teaching you that lesson. The version of me that you killed was nothing but a clone. I can't say the same about our friends, but that was the price we had to pay, and if they vote live, you might be stuck killing those clones forever."

"You're not making sense. Clones? But all the blood and screaming. It sounded just like you and-"

"I'm just good at what I do. It also wouldn't be much of a lesson if you realised it was a clone, would it?"

"But if they chose the live option, I know they're clones, so what's the point? Can't you just let me go? I have learned my lesson. I'm sorry, I really am!" Panic drowns me as his face is anything but empathetic.

"It's like you can't help but underestimate me." an alarm rings loudly, cutting him off. "Oh well, guess times up."

He's completely lost it. I've pushed him far from the edge, and now I'm paying for it.

"I hope you enjoyed the escape room because you'll do it again... and again until something breaks. And it will probably be you."

"Please don't do this", I plead, but his smile never leaves his face.

"See you in episode two, JJ." I struggle desperately once more and yell, but I can feel my consciousness start to fade again. I spout incoherent sentences in a desperate attempt to sway him, but his smile only grows as my vision turns black.

A cool breeze hits my body and body up, and the smell of stale rain assaults my nose. The feeling of a hard gravel floor stabs my back unforgivingly, but I don't feel like moving yet. I feel like I just had the worst dream ever. It felt so real and painful.

"JJ?" A familiar voice says. I open my eyes and see him staring back at me.

"Charlie, you're not dead!" Without thinking, I sit up and wrap my arms around him. I feel like crying.

"Dead? Why would I be dead? You just suddenly passed out when we got into the building." He looks at me worryingly.

Right, it must have been a dream.

"Come on, you need to be in top form if we are going to be able to do this escape room. Can't have you dragging us down, can we?" Charlie grabs my arms and pulls me to my feet. Sasha, Julia, Harry and Robert crowd me and look at me with relief before walking further into the building.

"How long was I out for?" I ask.

"Only like five minutes. Come on, let's go," Charlie replies as he pulls me along with them.

We walk up a set of stairs and then into a hall. A monitor and a set of watches sit on a table in the middle of the room. The monitor flickers on, and a figure appears.

"Welcome everyone to the first-ever livestream escape room."

CONSEQUENCES

Smile For The Camera Epilogue

My heart thumps painfully in my throat as I run up the stairs. He gradually increases the distance between us before stopping for a few seconds, causing a voice to echo uncontrollably in my head.

Catch him! Catch him!

I run faster. The staircase feels like it's going on forever, but I don't feel tired. Step after step, it feels like nothing's changing. I want to stop running, but my body doesn't let me. Anger boils through me as he finally gets closer and closer.

"Come on, Robby!"

My arm reaches out faster than my brain can process. I need to let him go.

I can't catch him; it will ruin my whole plan. Everything I worked so hard to create. I can't catch him, or he will die.

He can't die.

He needs to suffer.

My thoughts are instantly silenced as I lunge forward and tackle him to the floor.

"You did this to us, Robby."

Again.

I've had this same dream nearly every day for the past five years.

Five years ago, I wasn't able to sleep till I passed out.

Six years ago, I was living my best life.

Seven years ago, I was torturing my friends for the sake of revenge.

Now, I rely on sleeping pills more than water. I never fail to take more than double the recommended, which causes something to always be the hardest part of my day.

Waking up.

My eyes always refuse to cooperate with me, and my body stays paralysed so long after consciousness that it would be easy to mistake me for dead. Sometimes, I wouldn't be able to get up at all, like the weight of my guilt was holding me down. It caused me to dread going to sleep nearly as much as waking up. However, since every day of my life is the same, I still try to spend as little time awake as possible.

I don't have a nine-to-five because I don't need any more money. I don't have any friends because I got rid of them, and I accomplished everything I wanted in life.

However, if anyone were to ask me if it was worth it, the answer would be simple.

No, it wasn't.

At that moment, it felt great. It felt justified. It felt like I was the true hero punishing the villains, but I see that now, in the harsh light of my lonely reality, and I've had a few years to feel the full effect of it.

Their faces flash constantly in my mind, all the good times that we had instantly followed by their distraught faces on camera as they experience their final moments as well as their friends.

I shouldn't feel guilty for what I did; I have no reason to.

At least, that's what I used to think. Then I constantly thought about handing myself in to the police, admitting that the whole thing was real and that I really tortured and killed my friends just to get back at someone I hated.

What's stopping me?

Simple.

It's the tiny part of me that still thinks I was justified. I hate myself for it, but the feeling won't go away no matter how hard I try and trust me, I have tried everything.

I stare at the ceiling, allowing my thoughts to run where they please. My whole body aches as I reach over to my bedside table and grab the small white bottle, attempting to use as little effort as possible. I flip open the cap and pour four pills into my mouth, swallowing them with ease. I take a sip of water from the bottle I've left by my side for about a week. I unsuccessfully try to be careful, creating a small pool beneath my head that gradually turns comforting. Eventually, my thoughts slow down, and my mind feels heavy. I allow myself to drift into my most familiar state—back into the dream that haunts me.

A loud knock at the door pulls me out of my dream. Nothing has ever gotten me out of a dream before the end, no matter what. I continue to lie still as the knocking persists; I can't think of a single person who would be here to see me, which gives me a bad feeling.

The knocking continues for another ten minutes, so I reluctantly swing my legs out of bed, preparing to finally stand up. The knocking matches my increasingly loud and painful heartbeat; my body feels heavy, and my head pounds mercilessly, forcing me to move at a sloth's pace.

I finally reach the door and swing it open, desperate for the knocking to stop. I squint at the figure standing before me as the bright lights in the corridor attack me.

"Hey, Robby." A sharp pain erupts through my entire body as his voice echoes in my head. My heart aches, and I instinctively take a step back. Every part of my body begs me to run, shut the door, or do anything back, but I can't move any further. My mouth feels dry, but I finally manage to speak after a long, awkward silence,

"How are you…" I trail off as a lump forces its way into my throat.

"Alive?" He cuts me off and steps towards me, holding the door open with his hand, forcing me to retreat.

"But… I killed you." A sour taste fills my mouth as the words escape me. He scoffs at me and crosses his arms, stepping closer to me.

"No, Robby, you left me to die. You were just so full of yourself. You thought there would be no holes in your plan, but there were a few, and you didn't actually check that I was dead, did you?" A slight smirk creeps onto his face as I struggle to process what is happening.

I try to speak up, but I can't. I want to ask how he's alive and for him to stop calling me Robby, but the more he talks, the more conflicting emotions swirl within me—a mixture of guilt, remorse, and something even more potent.

Fear.

The type of fear that paralyses you and makes you feel like you have lost all of your five senses. The kind of fear that instantly makes you lose all train of thought.

"Hey buddy, it's okay. I'm here now, and I'm willing to forgive you." He looks me up and down, thinking for a moment. The smirk on his face vanishes and is quickly replaced with a sincere smile. "You know what? I'll do you one better."

He walks around the room, picking up items and analysing them for a few seconds before putting them down again.

"I know how much the guilt has been tearing you apart. I have the perfect way for you to overcome it. You just gotta do something for me." He stops walking around and looks at me. The lump in my throat suddenly disappears. Anger clouds my mind as I walk directly up to him.

"Do something for you? You haven't changed at all. You're still trying to walk all over me, aren't you? This is exactly why I tried to…! To…" The lump in my throat reappears almost as suddenly as it disappeared. He looks down at me. I can't tell if it's a smug or sincere look, but it immediately stops my thought process.

"Tried to kill me?" He folds his arms as he finishes my solemn sentence. My usual guilt amplifies tremendously as I look into his eyes momentarily. Memories of those days flood my brain like heavy fog.

All the monitors lined up in a row, happily watching all of my friends suffer and die because I thought they were expendable.

"You can't even look me in the eyes. I know you think about it all the time. How it felt good at the time; how you were so proud of yourself till it all sank in, and you realised how fucked up it was." The smile is evident through his tone, and I feel his gaze piercing my skull. The weight of my conscience becomes even more difficult to bear because he is precisely correct.

That's what happened.

"How did you know?" I try to sound confident, but my voice wavers uncontrollably, and I can't tell he's not buying my facade.

"Because I know you, Robby. Even though you hate me, I don't hate you. That's why I'm here, to give you the opportunity to make peace with your conscience." He turns away from me again and starts walking around the room, picking up random items and inspecting them thoroughly.

"I only hated you because you went out of your way to make my life miserable! You hung around our group only to torment me. You tore our group apart!" I feel the anger boiling up inside me again as I watch him effortlessly spout his bullshit. He makes it seem like he's the victim here.

"If that's the case, how come out of our entire group, I'm the only one still alive? Think what you want, but I adored that group. The only one that tore it apart was you! I'm not the one that killed them. You are. How can you even live with yourself knowing that all this fancy stuff you've got is because you manipulated, tortured and killed your friends? Over and over again." He picks up a glass ornament and slowly lets it slip from his hand. " All of this was bought with the money you made off that show while living in a shitty flat. It's like you're trying to let everyone on the outside know that you're guilty while secretly living in luxury." He grabs two more ornaments and lets them slip gracefully out his fingers. They smash loudly on the ground, forcing my body to flinch.

I want to move, yell, and stop him, but I can't. The rage I felt drains quickly out of me as I realise something important.

He's right.

Not only did I sacrifice my friends to get revenge on one person, but that person happens to be the only one still breathing. The only person who's not a victim here is me. Those years of planning, working, and executing were all for nothing.

Sasha.

Julia.

Harry.

Charlie.

They all died for nothing. I accomplished nothing but self-inflicted psychological torture. JJ looks unaffected while I'm here, losing my mind every fucking night because of it.

That's right. If he seems fine, maybe I should listen to him. I can put this whole thing behind me. It may all start with his forgiveness.

"Stop. I'll listen to you. What do you want me to do?" It's obvious I'm close to tears; no amount of acting could hide it.

He gently places the ornament he was about to drop on the table and walks towards me again, putting his hands comfortingly on my shoulders.

"Hey, hey, calm down. Relax. It's only something straightforward, okay?" He shakes me slightly, trying to get me to look at him, but I can't. My guilt is at an all-time high right now. Every time I look at him, I see and hear everything. I'm a terrible person. This is the very least I can do. "I learned that the best way to get over trauma is to relive it."

He puts an arm around my shoulder and pulls me to the kitchen. He starts opening and closing draws and cupboards in quick succession.

"Relive it? I relive it every night," I mutter, "What are you looking for?" I'm struggling to figure out where this is going.

He opens the final draw and stops.

"The only way to get rid of your guilt is to finish what you started, Robby." JJ pulls out a large kitchen knife and turns towards me with a sincere and kind smile.

"What…" I try to take a step back, but my body feels paralysed even as he walks towards me, his calm smile never leaving his face. My heart beats hard in my throat, alarm bells echoing in my head as he gets closer, but I can't do anything.

Is this how they felt? So scared they can't move.

"What's the matter with you? I can't kill you." He turns the knife handle to me, waiting for me to take it. "You're going to kill me."

My hands stay firmly by my side. I can only shake my head as my feet stay glued to the floor.

"Get away from me with that." Tears start to fall down my cheeks as images of the games flash harshly in my mind.

"You were too much of a bitch to do it yourself, so you made me do it. Every time I made it to the end of the 'games', every time I thought I would get out only to be back at the start again."

The calm look on his face completely disappears as I finally look him in his eyes. I manage to take a step back, but he grabs my arm and forces my hand to grip the handle of the knife, holding it there tightly as he allows the blade to press against his chest.

"Stop it, are you insane! I don't want to kill you. Why would you want me to kill you?!" I desperately try to pull my hand off the knife, but he holds on tighter, making it start to hurt.

"Come on, Robby, this is the only way for you to get over your guilt. Finish what you started." His tone sounds...

Happy?

No.

He's mocking me.

Why is this happening?

I've been tormented by nightmares for years, and now I feel like I'm living in one. I can't let JJ die. I can't deal with any more guilt.

"JJ, stop! I'm sorry. Please stay alive!" I try to reason with him, desperately trying to pull my arm away, but I stumble into the table.

A loud crash echoes in the room as another glass ornament falls to the ground, forcing my body to flinch again.

"Your half-assed apology won't bring anyone back!" JJ yanks my hand harder, causing the knife to start forcing its way past his skin. He doesn't yell, wince or cry.

He just looks at me.

"Goodbye, Robert." He quickly steps forward and pulls my hand closer until it touches his chest, the metal caressing my once steadily beating heart.

My heart?

Why is my heart hurting?

I can't feel my legs.

I look down and see a red pool flooding the floor. Is that coming from me? The knife is still in JJ's chest, but no blood is coming out of him. I want to ask him what's happening, but the only thing that escapes my mouth is a cough.

Then another.

Then another.

I can't stop.

Why can't I stop?

My body becomes too heavy for my legs, so I slump to my knees, the knife finally slipping from my hand. My vision becomes blurry, and I feel like I'm coughing my organs out. Bright crimson spills out of my mouth like a waterfall. My eyes dart rapidly around the room. I need help, but something is missing.

Where did JJ go?

He's not here anymore.

I can't keep myself up anymore. I feel myself fall forward; I can't stop myself. The pool surrounds my head, and a beautiful crimson red becomes the only colour I can see.

It's warm and weirdly comforting, like when I spilt hot water on my pillow. However, this is nicer. It's like my body is submerged in warmth; it makes me feel calmer by the second. I allow my eyes to close, letting my sense of touch take the reins.

This feels so nice. I'll get JJ to try it sometime.

MENTAL

A view from the window greets me. In the distance, birds fly across the cyan sky, clouds move slowly and calmly, and the sea glistens in the bright sunlight as the slight aroma of salt finds its way to me. Behind me, the door swung open. Hunter, my best (and only) friend, is standing in the doorway, smiling.

"Kovu, you'd better hurry up, or your food will get cold. Hurry up and come downstairs," he says as he turns on his heel and goes downstairs. I follow closely behind.

As we arrived in the dining room, the smell of pancakes and bacon fly happily in the air. We sit down at the table and start to eat. We eat, talk and laugh without a care in the world but we lose track of time. I glance outside the window to see grey clouds, heavy rain, rough ocean waves and not a single bird in sight. Then, there was a knock at the door. Hunter nods his head in the direction as he starts to clean the table and wash up. I reluctantly get up and trudge towards the door. Who could be all the way out here in this tragic weather?

I grab the door handle and pull it open. A tall man stands there in the pouring rain with a black umbrella. He is wearing a suit and dark glasses. Seems like something in a movie. He looked at me with a stern face and asked,

"Are you Kovu Devland?"

"Yeah, who's asking?" I reply, sceptically

"You're going to have to come with me." He suddenly grabs my arm and pulls me towards a black car waiting ahead.

"I'm not going anywhere with you!" I try to pull my arm away but his grip tightens and he pushes me in front of him and cuffs my hands behind me. Definitely something out of a movie.

What did I do to deserve this? I call out for Hunter but I'm only met with silence.

The strange man opens the back door and pushes me inside. Two people are at the front dressed the same as the man I saw first. He jumps into the car and sits next to me, slamming the door as he does. The car jolts forward at a frightening speed, leaving my home behind.

The person in the passenger seat turns to face me, reaches into their pocket and pulls out a blindfold. They reach forward and try to put on my head. I thrash around making it near impossible to put it on. They reach into their pocket again and pull out a gun. My body freezes.

"Don't even think about trying anything" they warn as they point it at me. I obey, stilling my movements, allowing the blindfold to be tied around my head, swallowing my vision with darkness.

If I took the gun, I could have shot the driver and the man next to me before shooting the one in the passenger seat. What am I thinking? I could never shoot or kill anyone. To escape, I could use the feel of the car turning to get back home. I just have to remember which way it's going in case I get away from these people. Left, right, right, fourth exit of a roundabout. Yes, if this continues like this, I could make it back.

The car finally stops. I remember nothing. Great.

"Get out!" The man next to me shouts as he pulls on my arm, dragging me into the rain. He tugs harder at my arm as we walk to what I can only assume is the place they are going to keep me. My wet clothes stick dreadfully to me. The sound of rain hitting the floor and rapid footsteps echo loudly in my ears till we finally reach a stop. I hear a gate swing open followed by a large bolted door.

My blindfold is forcefully pulled off, and the ceiling lights blind me. When my eyes finally adjust, I look around at my new surroundings. There is a big curved desk in the corner, a few chairs in the middle of the room, glass walls down a long corridor, and... People? They are people, but they look and act strange. Some seemed normal enough to socialise with, but others stood alone with fierce, menacing, scary, or scared looks on their faces.

The suited man pushes me towards the curved desk. There's a large woman behind it typing at a computer. Without looking up she spoke,

"Name and age?"

The man whispers something to the woman that makes her abruptly stop typing and look up at me in horror. What have I done? My name can't be that bad, can it?

"Is he the one that-" The woman stammers. The man next to me simply nods. She shakily picks up the phone and dials a number. Five, six, eight, eight. I don't know why but that number seems familiar. Probably just saw it somewhere.

"He's here sir" the woman mumbles into the phone. After a little while, she puts the phone down and talks to the kidnapper in a hushed whisper. I didn't focus on the conversation but I can make words like "deserved" and I think the word "Manburg"? Another thing that seems familiar. Oh well. My focus is on the entrance, soon to be my exit. I watch as another suited man approaches the door, puts a key in the lock and turns it twice. An audible click erupts in the room as he slides a bolt at the top of the door and swings it open. This could be my chance to escape while my personal guard was distracted. I make a break for it.

The door gets closer to closing. I hear the guard shout out but I keep running. The handcuffs are making it near impossible for me to pick up more speed. Even so, I'm close to making it. I'm only a few feet away from freedom... BANG! I freeze in my tracks, the door slamming closed inches in front of me. I was so close.

All adrenaline drains from my body and that's when I feel it. A stinging in my leg. I look down to see a scarlet pool leaking it, painting my shorts red. My vision starts getting darker and blurry as I collapse to the floor. Footsteps vibrate against my ear, the noise echoes in my head for a while before they finally stop. I faintly see the guard standing over me with a smug smile, holding a gun loosely in his hand.

He crouches down in front of me and whispers into my ear sadistically,

"You nearly made it but no inmates touch this door, let alone leave. Especially psychopaths like you." Inmate? Psychopath? I'm neither of those things, right? Yeah, I haven't done anything wrong. I try to open my mouth to protest but I can only let out a gasp in response.

Who knew being shot was so bad. I try to hold onto my consciousness but it slips away and my vision goes completely black.

An ice-cold shock wakes me; water drips down my face. I cough and splutter, then hear faint laughter around me. I try to wipe my face, but I can't move my arm. Opening my burning eyes, I see my arms stretched out beside me, my legs straight down both chained to a wall. Despite knowing it was a lost cause, I try to wiggle my way out, which only increases the laughter to an uproar. I try to compose myself as I look around. Bright lights fill my eyes, and the smell of popcorn fills the air.

The wooden floor below me cuts off a few metres in every direction. Am I on a stage? Why is this happening to me? Why is there such loud laughter?

My racing thoughts are cut off as a cracking sound echoes in the large room, and a large figure looms over me. His colossal build blocks the blinding light as he looks down at me. His eyes are suffused with hatred, and a wide, evil grin splits his face.

"Let me hear you scream, psychopath." He mocks as he raises his right arm, a whip firmly in his hand. The pandemonium from the invisible crowd picks up again. He swings his arm down hard, the whip slapping against my stomach. My wet clothes increase the pain immensely as it shoots through me in an instant. Screams escape my mouth involuntarily as it happens again and again. Clapping, shouting and cheering. My vision blurs as tears fill my eyes. What did I do to deserve this?

Another bucket of water slowly pours down my face, causing the crowd to laugh and cheer again. I try to move my head from side to side to escape the slow-falling water, which makes the crowd laugh harder and cheer louder. The water stops.

Then, there's a spark. I raise my head to see the man grinning even more as he raises his left hand. In it is a black taser that he sparks again but closer to me. However, he takes a few steps back. Maybe he has a heart, after all. I think? He crouches down and points at the floor with it. I look down at the wooden floor and see my feet in a pool of water. That explains the water obsession. I try to raise my feet out of the water; it's too late. The man presses the auto button on the taser and drops it into the water.

The electricity runs through my body, making me feel lifeless and helpless. I try to grip onto the strands of my sanity with very little success. A hoarse scream escapes me. Then, despite my efforts, my vision goes black once again.

I'm alive? Why? How? Forcing my eyes open, I look around. As my vision clears, I can see: a small, low dirty bed; a large, secure door with a small rectangle box above that brings in a tiny amount of light and dark painted brick walls.

Feeling groggy, I try to stand up. I'm forcefully dragged back down by my chained arms and ankles. I look down and see a metal cage around my mouth. Well, this is degrading. I try to shake it off, but it stays firmly on my face. I try to scream but my throat is sore, and only a meek whisper is let out.

Suddenly, the jingle of keys disrupts the silence. The door swings wide open, and a blinding light slowly fills the room. I squeeze my eyes shut to avoid it, and that's when I hear a familiar voice.

"Hey there, friend, how are you holding up?" I turn to face the direction of it. A figure is standing in the doorway, smiling—just like this morning. "Deja vu, no?" He laughs as he approaches me and crouches to my eye level.

"Did you do this to me, Hunter? You're my best friend!"

"Of course not. You did this to yourself. You deserve this, and as if I could ever be friends with a psychopath like you. You did all that and got off scot-free because nobody was there to make you atone. Except me. Years later. I've finally done it."

"What did I ever do to you?"

"Well, I guess I do have to remind you. Later though. I'm going to make you feel all the pain you put everyone through, especially Elijah." Hunter pulls a knife from his pocket. He takes off the cage and presses it lightly against my cheek. He starts pushing it, causing me to grit my teeth and glare into his eyes as I struggle to stop myself from yelling.

He pushes the knife harder into my skin as he trails it down my arm, leaving a leaking red line behind. After doing the same to the other arm, he slips the knife back into his pocket. My arms are throbbing, and my head is pounding. Without another word, Hunter walks out the door. Maybe he felt bad? He is my best friend, after all.

Wrong again.

Soon after, he comes back holding a large black bag.

"You see, Kovu. These years living under the same roof as you were the most painful years of my life. Every time I saw you, flashes of everything you did flooded my mind. I spent those years planning for this moment." His grin widens as he starts to open the bag. "Don't faint too quickly now."

I'm the victim here. This shouldn't be happening!

Hunter tortured me for hours on end.

Anytime I'm close to fainting, ice-cold water is dumped onto me.

"I don't feel like reminding you today. I'll be back tomorrow." He leaves, locking the door behind him.

Burns, cuts and bruises cover my body. Tears prick my eyes at the thought of this happening again. I won't be able to bear it. I cry for ages till sleep finally grabs me.

Days, weeks and months pass by painfully slowly. It's the same nearly every day. Sometimes, he would leave me for a day or two so I could stir in my own brain and paranoia. It made me miss him till the cycle started again. Torture after torture. Hour after hour. Each time different from the last, equally as painful or slightly more. Never less. How am I still alive?

"I think it's time I showed you a little something." He reached behind him and picked something up. It was a book with a smiley face carved into it. Images flashed through my mind in an instant, none of them are good.

I did that? It can't have been me. There's no way. I can't have! But…

I did. Yes. I so did. None of them are good, for them. I feel a smirk growing on me

"By the look on your face, you remember right, psychopath?"

"Oh, I remember now. Nice to see you again, Jay. You finally got that backbone, huh?."

THE PERSONAL BLOODSHED

The Mental Prequel

Twilight was starting to arrive and blood-thirst was high. It was going to end quicker than it had started. Everything was reaching its end game for all the people. Two sides that could never merge as one. A fight for ultimate power and anarchy. However, it was an effortless battle.

Newburg was a small country with a population of around 2000 patriotic civilians. On the 22nd of december, it was announced that Alan was the new president and Elijah, Kovu's childhood friend, was chosen as his vice president just to spite him. With the new power, it had already gotten to the leaders head as he could finally settle a long term feud he had. Pretty childish of him.

"Well Kovu, I have been waiting a long time for this. You're banished from this country you tyrannical bastard."

Kovu was instantly exiled and happily forgotten by everyone he thought loved as he was dragged out. Everyone except Elijah.Kovu knew that Alan hated him for a long time but didn't think he would go this far, he was almost impressed.

After what felt like hours of wandering outside of his ex-country, Kovu found an isolated building in a Tundra, north of Newburg.

It was a large cottage made out of wood and surrounded by bright lights. A blanket of snow coated the roof and stairs that went along the side of the house. Kovu walked up the stairs to the door, admiring the beauty of the house. He knocked on the door. No reply. He knocked again. Still no reply.

He walked backwards and spotted the open window. How convenient. He looked around for a way to get up. Almost immediately he came up with a plan. He climbed onto the bannister that surrounded the snowy stairway then climbed up the drainpipe. Fairly simple really. The snow caused almost no issues as he climbed up silently, made it to the window and climbed through.

He stepped into a large bedroom. The plain white walls were covered in scenery photos along with some war related one's; the wooden floor was mostly covered in soft, red carpet and the bookshelf was filled with some interesting looking books from fiction to nonfiction.

Kovu walked towards the door and grabbed the door handle and swung it open only to see a man standing there. He had a small shiny object in his hand as he held an offensive pose. He had dark skin, long black hair, a bit taller than Kovu's six foot two height and was quite built. Kovu held his hands up in defence and smirked as he saw the person standing before him. The man could only frown in response, not pleased with the sudden intrusion.

"You weren't exactly the quietest climbing the pipe, were you Kovu? Anyway, shouldn't you be with your little

Governmental country or whatever?" He said, rolling his eyes but keeping the weapon pointed at him.

Ignoring the shady comment, Kovu replied, "Not my country anymore."

"They finally couldn't wait to see the back of you, eh?" the man scoffed and rolled his eyes again but lowered his weapon.

"I want you to help me take it back," Kovu said, bluntly.

"Take it back?" He repeated, "so you can go back to your unfair hierarchy and corruption? I don't think so, I'm going to destroy it all now that you're out the way. You could always help me." Kovu thought for a moment, wondering if it was necessary to get rid of Newburg.

The thought of somebody else in power, especially somebody he despised, increased his anger. Maybe it would be better if it was gone. However, his legacy…

That in all honesty, he didn't care about.

Finally, he concluded.

"I want to help you destroy Newburg, Kailen"

"That's more like it," Kailen says, putting his weapon away. "I'm only choosing to trust you because I know that you're not truly on the side of the government despite your family tree. This also just benefits me massively. However, if you start another government I will destroy everything you love." Kovu just smiled and nodded dramatically before telling him everything he knew about the new rulers of Newburg.

After continuous nagging, Kailen finally agreed to let Kovu stay with him until their revolution. He knew that it would be easier to plan like this but he didn't trust Kovu. He was the only one who knew what he was truly like and what he could do. He definitely didn't want that opposing him, it would make his plan and guaranteed failure.

This plan was very simple. Blow up Newburg. However, it was way easier said than done. He didn't have any explosives. He had nearly all the weapons under the sun for close and long-distance combat but zero explosives. Kovu had a solution to that problem. Although he had a solution, there was still a problem. Kovu had stacks of explosives in his basement in case of emergencies. Problem solved right? Wrong. The basement was in his house which was in the middle of Newburg and Kovu wasn't allowed there. They thought hard about how they would get the stuff from the centre of the country, all the way back to the Tundra. Their minds were blank and hope was starting to wither away.

Suddenly, there was a knock on the door. The two exchanged glances before slowly making their way to the door. They both picked up one of the axes that were hanging on the wall, holding it firmly in one hand. Kailen reached for the door handle as Kovu positioned himself on the other side. He swung it open to see a small male with fluffy brown hair. He saw the weapons and held his hands up trying to show his passiveness. Kovu poked his head around the door.

"Heeeeey!" Kovu exclaimed as he dropped the axe to the floor and embraced the man. "What are you doing here, Elijah?" Kovu gripped his shoulders lightly and held him at arm's length, looking into his distressed eyes.

"I'm glad I found you, I was worried about you after you were banished," Elijah responded earnestly. Kovu and Elijah chatted for a while, Kailen just stood there silently feeling slightly sceptical of the new person.

"So how do you know each other so well?" Kailen eventually spoke out.

"We've been friends since we could walk," Kovu exclaimed as he wrapped his arm around Elijah's shoulder, pulling him closer to him, grinning from ear to ear. Kailen only glared at Kovu and his carefree nature. He grabbed his wrist and pulled him away from Elijah.

"You're not thinking of including him in our revolution are you?" Kailen questioned.

"Of course I am. If I can trust anyone, it's Elijah." Kovu said enthusiastically.

"This is a stupid idea. You just told me he's the bloody vice president!" Kailen whispers angrily as he rubs the bridge of his nose in annoyance. "Don't mess this up Kovu and send him away." He turns around and goes upstairs to his bedroom. Kovu turned to Elijah, his smile transforming from friendly to evil. A small chill ran down the newcomer's spine as he saw the sudden seriousness in his eyes.

"The president is going down," Kovu whispered before pulling Elijah into the planning room. He explained their plan but not their true explosive plan. He told him that they were going to poison him.

When he agreed to be a double agent for them Kovu sent him on his way and went to bed.

Today is the day. The day they go to the Newburg centre to retrieve the most important part of their plan. Kailen and Kovu were up at the crack of dawn prepping for their mission while Elijah went to complete his part of the plan.

Normally, he would have to stay by the president's side as his second in command, however, the president was very lazy and often passed out from drinking so Elijah could wander around by himself. His constant intoxication made it easy to pass off laws and plans as they were often replied to with effortless nods of agreement. The new plan Elijah had gotten signed off on is to have a town festival, inviting all citizens to a mandatory arrival in a week's time. He didn't really get why but he didn't want to disappoint Kovu. Elijah was getting fresh air as he walked around the town centre, planning decorations for the party. That's when he bumped into someone. They dropped the notebook they were writing in and it glided across the concrete floor. He looks up but quickly looks away, avoiding all eye contact.

"I'm so sorry about that, I wasn't looking where I was going." The man says in a meek tone as he looks around for his notebook. Elijah picks it up but it's quickly snatched away from him by the shy guy. "Sorry, I didn't mean to take it from you like that. This book is really important to me. I'm Jay" he extended a hand slowly and Elijah shook it.

"It's alright, calm down. I'm Elijah, what's the book for?" Elijah asks as he sees him writing something in the book again. He reads it from upside down, 'I bumped into Elijah. I think he's the vice president. He seems nice'.

Jay mumbles something inaudible to Elijah still staring at the ground then quickly says "I have to go" before scurrying past Elijah into his house that was a few metres away. Elijah shrugged it off and decided to go back to the Tundra feeling weirded out by the meeting.

When he arrived, Kailen opened the door with an axe in hand again. He relaxed as he saw Elijah standing at the door. Kailen steps aside to let Elijah in then closes the door behind him. Kovu came out of the door leading to the basement/ planning room and greeted Elijah with a hug before asking him if he had any news.

"There will be a town party this time next week in the town centre and everyone will be there on a mandatory arrival" Elijah explains

"That's perfect, the TNT will be placed by then."

"I also met a strange guy. He writes down everything in a notebook. I think he has memory problems like my mum. Not that it matters to you guys."

"No no, I'm intrigued. Do you know where he keeps it? " Kovu says, staring blankly back at Elijah.

"Probably in his house, which strangely has only one door separating yours and his on the left. Why do you want to know?" Elijah responded hesitantly

"No reason just striking up a conversation. Anyway, are you ready to go, Kailen?" Kovu says reassuringly.

"Of course I am, I've been waiting for you" Kailen responds tiredly. Kovu laughs and walks past both Kailen and Elijah at the front door. He's about to open the door before Kailen calls his name.

"what are you doing?"

"going to get the thing, what else?" Kovu retorted sarcastically

"We aren't just going through to Newburg, neither of us are very welcome there. We are going under it." Kailen states as he walks down to the basement. He pressed a button on the bottom of the planning table and part of the floor in the back corner started to open revealing a set of stairs that lead downwards. Kailen took an axe off the wall and put on an oversized hoodie.

Kovu copies his actions and they go down the steps. Elijah decides to go back to Newburg and plan for the festival from above ground.

Kailen led the way through a large underground tunnel that was both tall, wide and well lit.

"Did you build this?" Kovu asked as he admired the newfound surroundings.

"You could say that it's been passed down for a few generations," Kailen answered, subtly dismissing the topic.

"Does it go under all of Newburg?" Kovu says ignoring Kailen's desire for silence

"mhm," Kailen responds with a monotone voice.

After around 20 minutes of silent walking, Kailen abruptly stopped in his tracks. Kovu looks at the ladder tower upwards and the sign next to it reads 'Kovu's house'. Though deeply disturbed and concerned, he followed Kailen up the ladder.

"I'm going to bring this up later by the way" Kovu mumbled. Kailen only rolled his eyes as he opened the trap door above them and climbed into the room above. He was forced into a crouched position as he felt the wooden planks above him. Kovu climbed up and crouched then watched in curiosity at the next step. Kailen felt a certain spot repeatedly before retracting his arm back and bawling up a fist. Before Kovu realised what he was going to do, Kailen swung his arm up with force breaking the floorboards above easily. He climbed through it as Kovu stared in awe at the strength and unnecessary damage to his house before eventually following him.

Chests filled the next room from wall to wall. As Kovu opened them his eyes lit up in excitement. Each chest was full to the brim with blocks of TNT.

"I have a plan for setting these off but the escape plan is not as concrete unless you don't mind losing your house or the tunnel," Kovu suggests

"The house is left untouched," Kailen says sternly.

"Fine then, new plan." Kovu shared his new plan with Kailen. Place TNT under all of Newburg in the tunnels far enough from the house that it won't affect it. Kailen was sceptical about this plan but agreed anyway. To place all the TNT and hook it up together may take a few days so they went back to the tunnels and started straight away. Well, Kailen did.

"Hey Kailen, is there a 'Jay's house' sign here by chance," Kovu asked. Kailen looked at him questionably but pointed to the left of Kovu's house. He thanked him and walked to the house.

He looked at the sign that read Jay's house and went up the ladder. He opened the hatch above him and looked up. He was in a vent shaft. He pulled himself up into it and started to crawl toward the light source coming from around the corner. He looked through the gate and saw what looked like a living room. Kovu weaved his hand through the grate and unlatched it on both sides. After he gently pushed the grate out he stepped out and stood in the neatly organised room.

Books were placed neatly on the shelves, the fireplace burned brightly with a nice orange glow and the sofas had square cushions placed precisely on the end seats. Pictures of calming backgrounds cover the pale walls and a fluffy rug laid across the wooden floor.

Kovu made his way towards the door. He grabbed the door handle and slowly pulled it open before stepping into the hallway. More paintings cover the walls. He creaked up the stairs, holding onto the railing for stability.

There were three doors in the oval-shaped landing. He went into the closet door to be met with a spare bedroom. The walls were plain, the bed had sheets neatly folded on top and a small TV sat in the corner of the room. He went to the next room. The bathroom. A surprisingly pleasant aroma greeted him. The bathroom was in the middle of the room, with a toilet and sink to the right and a stand-in shower to the left. He went to the final room.

He slowly pushed the handle and sneaked into the room. A shelf stood a few feet in front of him, on it was a bunch of scenery pictures. As he walked further in he could see more and more of the pictures, they covered the blue painted wall. Suddenly, Kovu's whole body froze.

A king-sized bed sat in the corner, a small cabinet next to it with a switched off lamp on top of it. A lump was formed the closer he got towards the bed. Elijah was in there. He had to be careful. He reached for the drawer and opened it. In it were a book and pen. It had a band over the top of it and was plain black. Kovu picked up the book, moved the band to the side and opened it. As he flicked through it his eyes beamed with hope. He picked up the pen and started writing in it.

After Kovu finished writing, he put them back where he got them. He was about to leave when he heard a cry for help. He looked back to see Elijah writhing around in his bed. Tears were forming in his eyes before they rolled down his cheeks and stained the pillow below him. Kovu watched in curiosity as he started calling out to someone.

"Mum! Mum, please don't do it!" Jay sobbed. He repeated it over and over before coming to a stop, only the sound of light snoring left his mouth. Finally, Kovu left the room and went back to the tunnel.

"What the hell have you been doing, I'm not doing this all by myself y'know?" Kailen questioned, feeling quite annoyed.

"Don't worry about it, you will thank me later for it anyway. Just trust me" Kovu replied, dismissing the conversation as he eventually helped Kailen with the TNT. He silently agreed to let the conversation go.

The next day in Newburg, Elijah was planning for the Newburg Festival aka The Doomsday Festival. Dark clouds loomed over the decorators as they put up posters and banners for the event. He saw Jay in the distance and decided to go and greet him. Elijah raised his hand in an attempt to wave but stopped halfway. He saw a look on Jay's face. A look of mild insanity and regret, his hair was messy, his clothes were creased and he clutched the black book tightly to his chest.

"Jay...?" Elijah looked at him, concerned. Jay jumped at the sudden speech directed at him and turned quickly in the direction it came from. He relaxed for a while before tensing again soon after as he looked at the Vice President. Elijah continued,

"What's the matter, you seem like you have seen a ghost"

"Nothing, I'm fine. Just didn't get much sleep last night." Jay replied, staring at the floor as he tried to dismiss the question. Elijah knew he was lying but didn't want to press any further.

"How about you hang out with me for a bit. You can help with the decorations or just relax if you want." Elijah watched as Jay's tense body relaxed once more and he nodded his head with a small smile.

They went off together down the pavement. Elijah mostly led the conversation but Jay listened intently, growing more and more comfortable with his new friend. They hung up decorations and posters, made music playlists then went to the town centre.

They went to a small coffee shop and ordered hot chocolate. When they got their drinks they sat at the outside table as the weather started to clear. They chatted for a long time, laughing and joking together. That's when it hit him. He had a job to do. Darkness had nearly engulfed the sky and he had to go back to the Tundra.

"Well. This has been fun Jay, really. I have some vice-presidential duties to do so I'll see you tomorrow. Yeah?" Elijah partially lied.

"Thank you for hanging out with me," Jay responded as they slowly parted ways with each other. Jay gripped onto his notebook and guilt welled up inside him as he slowly remembered what he had done.

Elijah started to make his way to the Tundra. He got a train most of the way there but had to walk for about forty-five minutes before arriving.

He knocked on the cottage door to be met with a smiling Kovu. He pulled him by the arm excitedly into the building and sat him down into the front room.

"Sooo, any new information?" Kovu asked

"Well, the festival preparations are coming along nicely. I made friends with Jay, he was in a bad state today. You didn't do anything to him yesterday, did you?" Elijah replied, sceptically.

"Of course not, I'm surprised you would even ask such a daft question." Kovu countered, standing up from the sofa. "I'm going back to help Kailen now, go back to your preparations."

With that, Kovu went down to the basement to assist his partner in crime. Once he travelled through the tunnel he finally saw Kailen.

"So, anything new?" He asked as he continued wiring the TNT.

"Nope, they are just setting up decorations and whatnot," Kovu replied and started helping again.

The rest of the day went by quickly along with the night. The next few days went by even quicker. Kailen noticed how Kovu's disappearances down the tunnel became more and more frequent. The number of times growing with his curiosity. He pushed his questions aside to focus on the explosive mission. Whether he did most of it himself didn't matter, he knew Kovu must have been doing something of value. At least he hoped.

The part of the tunnel under Newburg looked like a bomb site. Literally. Everything was basically done. They just had to wait for the festival which was only two days away.

The festival preparations were also nearly done. Stalls were set up everywhere, ribbons and banners were strung from houses and shops and a huge stage was set up in the centre of the small country, right outside Kovu's house, in front of a fountain. Elijah was tired but determined to help his friend so he made sure everything was perfect. That's when an idea hit him.

He went towards the tall building at the edge of the country, feeling confident in his plan. He arrived and knocked on the door. After a few minutes, the door swung open. There stood a tall man with a half-empty bottle of vodka in hand.

"Hello Mr President, there is something I would like to discuss with you," Elijah said. The tipsy man stared at him for a moment before taking a long sip of his drink. He turned around but left the door open for Elijah to follow and walked further into the large building.

They walked through an exquisite front hall and into a front room. It heavily contradicted the front of the building. It was messy. Alcohol bottles covered the floor, the sofas were out of line, pillows were thrown all over the place and the blank tv had a crack in it and was dripping with alcohol.

The president went and sat down on one of the sofas. Elijah sat on the one opposite him as he tried to avoid all of the mess.

"What do you want? I'm busy" the President complained.

"Well, I wanted to ask for a favour. Could you give a one day visit to Kovu? Just for the festival." Elijah said calmly.

"Festival, what festival?" The president asked, taking another long sip from the bottle.

"The one you signed and agreed to a week ago. All the preparations are up." Elijah motioned to the window. The president stumbled over and looked out at the decorations placed neatly around the country.

"Oh right. Sure whatever" He took out a pen and paper from a draw and messily wrote 'One day pass' across it. Elijah thanked him and scurried out of the house.

He made his way to the Tundra to tell Kovu the news. He felt happy knowing that he could help his friend take back his presidency.

He arrived at the cottage and knocked on the door like he's done many times. As it swung open, Kailen stood there with a noticeable scowl on his face.

"What do you want?" He asked.

"I got Kovu a one day pass for the festival" Elijah replied, beaming as he showed Kailen the paper.

"Ok, I'll just give it to him. We will be at the festival, see you then." Kailen said as he snatched the paper and slammed the door shut. Elijah stood there confused for a while before silently turning back home.

In the basement, Kovu was climbing back down a ladder that wasn't his own. Kailen got fed up with it and stormed over to him. He grabbed Kovu by his shirt and shouted,

"Kovu tell me what the hell you keep doing every night up there! I've placed most of TNT by myself then you told me to "cover for you" when Elijah came by-"

"Kailen, let go of me." Kovu cut him off. Kailen saw a menacing look spread across his face. A look that was anything but friendly. It startled him and he nearly backed down. He was physically stronger than Kovu but not by a lot. That's when Kailen remembered that they were surrounded by tons of TNT so getting into a fight would not be the best idea.

After a little while, Kailen lets go of Kovu with a small shove.

"I'll pretend that didn't happen. I will also tell you what I have been doing seeing as it bothers you so much." That he did and Kailen wished he never asked.

"But why would you-?" Kailen starts but is once again cut off by Kovu as a small chuckle escapes his mouth

"Because it is fun, Kailen. And because I can."

"You really are a psychopath Kovu"

"Yup, I know, " Kovu says as he starts to walk off down the tunnel towards the house. He reaches into Kailen's pocket and pulls out the paper then adds, "thanks for getting the door for me, I've got something else to do now" Kailen stood dumbfounded as he watched Kovu backwards wave at him.

It was the morning of the festival.

A few hours and a thousand people would be gathered in the town centre. Elijah was excited for Kovu to go back to being president instead of the current alcoholic. Feeling extremely optimistic, he went to find his newest friend. Jay.

Elijah practically skipped to Jay's house. Upon arriving, he could barely keep himself from smiling. He knocked on the door a few times and waited. When it was only replied to with silence, he knocked again a bit harder.

Silence.

"He's probably still on his morning walk" Elijah thought, feeling slightly disappointed. He decided to go and check up on all the preparations. He cursed a little under his breath as he looked up at the approaching light grey clouds.

"Stop struggling so much. You can't talk but you're still being extremely loud. We can't have Kailen hearing you now, can we?" Kovu said in a mocking but annoyed tone. He crouches down in front of the man sitting on a wooden chair so he could look him straight in his eyes. The man stared back without any anger in his eyes. It was only filled with fear.

Duck tape muffled his screams and chains restricted his movements. Despite his uncomfortable sleeping position he didn't give up on trying to get out.

"I didn't want to do this to you as you were such a great help to me." The man twitched slightly at that sentence as his eyes filled with panic. Loud muffled screams escaped him and he shook his head violently trying to deny the statement. Tears started to stream down his face but he stilled his movements.

I did this. I betrayed my own country. Why? I didn't do this. I must have done it. I wrote it. His mind raced but eventually came to terms with it.

Kovu took the tape off his mouth.

"I'm a traitor…" The man whispered.

"Yes, you are. However, I'm not a traitor as I have nobody in that country but you finally have somebody now, don't you?" Kovu snaked around him to stand behind the chair and rested his hands on it.

"Please don't hurt him, I beg you," the man stammered, trying to collect himself slightly.

"Of course not! You helped me so much, I wouldn't hurt the one and only person that cares about you, even though you did betray him." Kovu says, a smirk forming on his face as he can visibly see him shaking. " I'll even take all this stuff off, ok?"

Kovu removes all the chains that restrained him and helped the man off the chair.

"Come on, I'll show you what you helped me accomplish," Kovu said as he dragged him down to the basement. He pressed the button under the table and watched the secret door slide open.

After a long while of walking they reached it. Kovu pushed the man to go in front of him as they turned the corner. That's when he stopped. TNT covered the walls, floor and ceiling of the tunnel. There was hardly any place to walk.

"Don't worry, they won't go off until I press a button. It's fine." Kovu reassured though it did anything but reassure the man. Seeing the explosives terrified him. He started to back away but suddenly felt a firm grip on his shoulder.

"Now, if you tell anyone about this I'll tie you up in this room and press the button. Got it?" Kovu warned as he slightly dug his nails into him. The man felt all the oxygen in him slowly leave as he quickly nodded his head.

"Use your words, Jay."

"I promise I won't say a word."

Upstairs, Kailen was getting ready for the festival. A black hoodie was pulled over his grey t-shirt along with dark blue jeans and trainers. He slipped his phone into his back pocket and went down stairs. He sat on the sofa and switched on the TV, browsing through all the channels cause who doesn't like to relax on the sofa before committing mass terrorism.

After about an hour, Kovu walked through the door.

"Come on let's go, it's starting soon and i've got things to do," He said.

"Yup, coming." Kailen responded, his eyes not leaving the TV. Kovu walks up to him and grabs his arm, pulling him away from it. Kailen let out a sigh as he allowed himself to be dragged away from his comfort. They left the house and set off to Newburg.

In Newburg, people were starting to gather around the town centre. Some swayed to the music that was being played from the high-hanging speakers, others swarmed the food stalls or just wandered around the area. Elijah was one of the latter. He wanted to do one last look around for Jay before taking a trip to the President's place. He wanted to share his first festival experience with his newest friend.

Finally, Elijah saw Jay. He was profusely sweating and looked like he was going to faint. He approached him and placed a hand on his shoulder, in an attempt to comfort him.

This only freaked Jay out. Before turning around, he slapped Elijah's hand away in fear. Not only did it terrify Elijah, it made him worry. He looked Jay in his eyes as he tried to pry an answer out of him. Jay's eyes only filled with a little bit of water and ran away.

Elijah stood there in pure shock and confusion but he had to go to the president, so he left.

At the president's mansion, his mild drinking was disturbed by a knock at the door. He trudged over to it and swung it open. Kovu stood there with a massive grin on his face.

"What the hell are you doing here?" Alan said.

"Well, I've got some news that I think you want to know." Kovu replied as he steps into the house. Alan retreated backwards as he made an effort to keep some distance.

"You know your Vice President, Elijah. He has betrayed you. He has been praying on your downfall and is planning to assassinate you very soon. Just a warning."

"Why would I believe you?"

"Even though you hate me, I don't hate you enough for you to be killed." Kovu smiled earnestly as he left the house through the window.

With perfect timing, the door knocked.

Alan's mind was fuzzy, the alcohol was taking affect. He could properly think if a plan to deal with an attempted assassination. He decided on a simple solution.

He quickly went upstairs to his bedroom and pulled out a metal object from the bedside draw, placed it in the waistband of his trousers. He then made his way to the door.

He looked through the door's eyepiece. Elijah stood on the other side. He had a smile on his face and his hands deep in his pockets. The president reached for the door handle and pulled it open.

"Hey Mr. President, are you ready for the festival... What are you doing?" Panic slowly filled Elijah's voice and to his consternation, the president was obviously drunk off his mind.

He looked ahead at the intoxicated man but not only did he stare back. A small black pistol did too. He slowly started to raise his hands in defence but Alan only got closer to pulling the trigger so he left them in his pockets.

"How about you put it down? I bought something for you," Elijah tried to say calmly, but the tremble in his voice revealed the truth.

"Don't think I don't know your plans, you damn bi-"

"What are you talking about? I don't know what you're accusing me of here, I just want to give you something."

"Oh, I think you know very well what I mean," Alan switches off the safety and pulls the trigger.

The bullet hurtles through the air, and the sound of the gun rings in their ears but only for one of them. It landed straight through his skull in a split second.

Elijah can't even mutter a word before he slowly falls backwards, half his body leaving the mansion. He hits the floor with a slight thud, and his body goes fully limp. His eyes grew pale and his skin lost heat.

Alan reached into the lifeless man's pockets. He felt a sharp scratch and felt elated that he saved his own life. Furthermore, he couldn't believe his enemy had helped him. He looked for the handle, but he could find it. If anything, the knife felt very square. He grabbed the object and pulled it out quickly. His face plummeted as he saw what it was. A small card had the words "thank you" written in light blue letters. Inside the folded card it read "it's only been a week but I've seen what hard work you have done outside your drinking. Thank you"

Alan looked at what he did and instantly felt like vomiting. He dropped the card in panic as his hands shook violently. He lied, he lied, HE LIED!

He left out the back exit of the mansion and went towards the festival. He staggered down the path till he finally reached it. People were dancing, eating and looking at stalls. Alan looked around till his eyes locked with a certain brown haired male and stormed over to him.

"WHAT DID YOU DO TO ME!" Alan shouted as he grabbed him by the shirt.

"I don't know what you mean, would you care to elaborate?" Kovu said with a small smirk on his face. Fury controlled Alan's body as his fist connected with the side of Kovu's face. Repeatedly. He stumbled backwards, but the sly smile never left.

Everybody's eyes were fixated on the fight happening in the centre of town. Eventually, a group of people separated the two. Alan had tears streaming down his face and Kovu was spitting blood out his mouth. The president's suit was ripped and he was screaming at the top of his lungs,

"YOU FUCKING PSYCHO! YOU DID THIS, YOU DID THIS!" The music stopped.

"Did what Mr President? kill my own Vice President? But you're the one that pulled the trigger, are you not?" Kovu said extremely condescendingly which only increased Alan's rage.

The group of people that surrounded them broke out into mass discussion. Kovu looked around at confused, distraught and angry faces. But one face was the most expressive. Jay.

Tears flowed past his face, almost forming a puddle on the floor. His eyes were wide, his mouth was agape and his body trembled immensely.

"I would love to stay here and chat Alan but I've got to run. Enjoy the rest of the festival." Kovu bowed and disappeared into the bustling crowd before setting off sprinting.

Kailen watched in awe and confusion at what had just happened. He knew Kovu had done something for Elijah to get killed. But why? He thought back to the reason he gave for messing with Jay and figured it was the same. He doesn't care about anything. He doesn't care about anyone. Kailen knew he was bad but not this bad.

Jay had yet to move. Floods of emotions were destroying his mind but a tsunami of antagonism washed them all away. He was no longer shaking with fear and despair, it was purely out of resentment for Kovu.

On a small cliff just outside Newburg is where Kovu stood. He looked over the country he once ruled over with ease. About 1000 people stood in the centre, huddled and panicking. Perfect.

He crouched down by a large rock and moved it to the side. Below it was a hole with a briefcase inside. Kovu lifted it up slowly, being careful not to pull out the two wires coming out the back of it. He used his right hand to hold it on his lap and the other to hold the padlock.

"I won't let you do this."

Kovu turned his head to look at the direction the voice had come from. Jay stood there, his hands were clenched, eyes red and puffy and tear stains covered his face. Kovu gently put the case on the ground and stood up.

"Whatever do you mean, don't you want to finish what we started?" Kovu replied, freakishly calm. He started to walk closer to him so Jay instinctively took a small step back.

"No, it will kill all those innocent people. I'm here to stop you."

"Are you really?" He takes another step forward making Jay do the opposite. Kovu laughed, "How do you plan to do that, you're scared of me! How could you possibly stop me?"

Kovu swiftly lunged forward. Before Jay had any time to react, he was being punched in the stomach. Punch after punch, it carried on and on till he eventually collapsed to the floor, winded beyond repair. His head spun as he suppressed the urge to vomit. He clutched his torso as he felt his consciousness drain from his body.

"Come on Jay, don't you want to avenge your friend? Isn't that what you came here to do not cry like a little bitch? I bet Elijah's feeling really disappointed in you all the way from hell! I can't wait to see you grow a backbone" Kovu mocked, feeling no empathy for the people he has let alone about to hurt.

Jay wanted to punch him in the face. He wanted to kill him. But he was too weak, he couldn't do anything against his best friend's murderer. He still feared him.

Kovu reached into his back pocket and pulled out a gun.

"This is the same gun that killed Elijah, you know? How about I kill you as well with a bullet between your eyes..." Fear erupted within Jay. His life was about to be snatched from him and he couldn't even fight back. He truly felt powerless. "Nah I'm kidding, you can watch the fireworks from up here with me, you seem pure hearted enough." Kovu threw the gun aside, kneeled back down and put the case on his lap. He turned the number dials on the padlock.

Five, six, eight, eight.

The case clicked and he pulled it open. Inside was a bunch of wires, binoculars, a screen and a large button.

"Well this was fun. Those traitors deserved it" He pressed the button.

A countdown from five appeared on the screen and it quickly went down. Kovu took the binoculars and looked through them at the country below. He saw everyone still gathered in the centre by the fountain. He saw Kailen. He was actually doing something funny. He was beating up the President. Ha. Too bad it didn't matter, he was going to die too.

BOOM!

Debris flew everywhere, it was spectacular and beautiful.

It was so beautiful that I didn't even realise Jay stood up. Something must have snapped in him but he still did have enough backbone to shoot me, not at that moment anyway. The years of pretending we were best friends was a bit extreme though but I'll give him credit where credit is due. He was smart.

Well, either way. Hell isn't that bad. I've settled in nicely here. Glad I met Jay really even if it led to where I am now. I had fun messing with and killing everyone.

www.ingramcontent.com/pod-product-compliance
Lightning Source LLC
LaVergne TN
LVHW061558070526
838199LV00077B/7094